To Mark, who gives me ideas and love,
and to Diane Arico, editor extraordinaire
—S. W.

To Linda Pratt
—T. W.

Library of Congress Cataloging-in-Publication Data
Williams, Suzanne, date.
Old MacDonald in the city /
by Suzanne Williams ; illustrated by Thor Wickstrom.
p. cm.
Summary: Increasing numbers of different animals,
from one horse to ten ants, try to steal food from
Old MacDonald's corner food cart.
ISBN 0-307-10685-3 (alk. paper)
[1. City and town life—Fiction. 2. Street vendors—Fiction.
3. Animals—Fiction. 4. Counting. 5. Stories in rhyme.]
I. Wickstrom, Thor, ill. II. Old MacDonald had a farm. III. Title.
PZ8.3.W6793 O1 2002   [E]—dc21   2001033085

The illustrations for this book were created
with oils on Bristol board.

Old MacDonald in the City

by **Suzanne Williams**

illustrated by **Thor Wickstrom**

A Golden Book ■ New York
Golden Books Publishing Company, Inc.
New York, New York 10106

Old MacDonald had a cart,
E-I-E-I-O.
Beside his cart there stood ONE horse,
E-I-E-I-O.

With a *neigh-neigh* here
and a *neigh-neigh* there.

Here a *neigh*, there a *neigh*,
Everywhere a *neigh*-*neigh*.

Old MacDonald had a cart,
E-I-E-I-O.

Behind his cart there jumped TWO dogs,
E-I-E-I-O.

With a *bow-wow* here
and a *bow-wow* there.

Here a *bow*, there a *wow*,
Everywhere a *bow-wow*.

Old MacDonald had a cart,
E-I-E-I-O.

Above his cart there flew THREE crows,
E-I-E-I-O.
With a *caw-caw* here
and a *caw-caw* there.
Here a *caw*, there a *caw*,
Everywhere a *caw-caw*.
Old MacDonald had a cart,
E-I-E-I-O.

Around his cart
there prowled FOUR cats,
E-I-E-I-O.

With a *meow-meow* here
and a *meow-meow* there.

Here a *meow*, there a *meow*,

Everywhere a *meow-meow*.   Old MacDonald had a cart,
E-I-E-I-O.

Upon his cart there leaped FIVE squirrels,
E-I-E-I-O.
With a *chitter-chatter* here
and a *chitter-chatter* there.
Here a *chitter*, there a *chatter*,
Everywhere a *chitter-chatter*.
Old MacDonald had a cart,
E-I-E-I-O.

Beyond his cart there flocked SIX pigeons,
E-I-E-I-O.
With a *coo-coo* here
and a *coo-coo* there.
Here a *coo*, there a *coo*,
Everywhere a *coo-coo*.
Old MacDonald had a cart,
E-I-E-I-O.

About his cart buzzed SEVEN bees,
E-I-E-I-O.
With a *buzz-buzz* here
and a *buzz-buzz* there.
Here a *buzz*, there a *buzz*,
Everywhere a *buzz-buzz*.
Old MacDonald had a cart,
E-I-E-I-O.

And toward his cart
there flapped EIGHT geese,
E-I-E-I-O.

With a *honk-honk* here
and a *honk-honk* there.
Here a *honk*, there a *honk*,
Everywhere a *honk-honk*.
Old MacDonald had a cart,
E-I-E-I-O.

Below his cart there scurried NINE mice,
E-I-E-I-O.
With a *squeak-squeak* here
and a *squeak-squeak* there.
Here a *squeak*, there a *squeak*,
Everywhere a *squeak-squeak*.
Old MacDonald had a cart,
E-I-E-I-O.

Beneath his cart there crawled TEN ants,
E-I-E-I-O.
With a *skiddle-skaddle* here
and a *skiddle-skaddle* there.
Here a *skiddle*, there a *skaddle*,
Everywhere a *skiddle-skaddle*.
Old MacDonald had a cart,
E-I-E-I-O.

Old MacDonald had a cart,
E-I-E-I-O.
With a *neigh-neigh* here
and a *bow-wow* there,
With a *caw-caw* here
and a *meow-meow* there,

With a *chitter-chatter* here
and a *coo-coo* there,
With a *buzz-buzz* here
and a *honk-honk* there,
With a *squeak-squeak* here
and a *skiddle-skaddle* there.

Old MacDonald had a cart,
E-I-E-I-O.